WEATHER and CLIMATE

Watching Weather

Robin Birch

Marshall Cavendish
Benchmark

New York

This edition first published in 2010 in the United States of America
by Marshall Cavendish Benchmark.

Marshall Cavendish Benchmark
99 White Plains Road
Tarrytown, NY 10591
www.marshallcavendish.us

First published in 2009 by
MACMILLAN EDUCATION AUSTRALIA PTY LTD
15–19 Claremont Street, South Yarra 3141

Visit our website at www.macmillan.com.au or go directly to www.macmillanlibrary.com.au

Associated companies and representatives throughout the world.

Library of Congress Cataloging-in-Publication Data

Birch, Robin.
    Watching weather / by Robin Birch.
        p. cm. – (Weather and climate)
    Summary: "Discusses why people watch weather, what they observe, how they collect data, and what that data can tell us"–
Provided by publisher.
    Includes bibliographical references and index.
    ISBN 978-0-7614-4470-1
    1. Weather forecasting–Juvenile literature. 2. Weather–Juvenile literature. I. Title.
    QC995.43.B57 2009
551.63–dc22

2009004978

Edited by Kylie Cockle
Text and cover design by Marta White
Page layout by Marta White
Photo research by Legend Images
Illustrations by Gaston Vanzet

Printed in the United States

Acknowledgments
The author and the publisher are grateful to the following for permission to reproduce copyright material:
Front cover photograph: Telescopes in the Dark Sector at Amundsen-Scott South Pole Station courtesy of National Science
Foundation, photo by Calee Allen
Photos courtesy of:
AAP/AP Photo/Ajit Solanki, **30**; © Alain/Dreamstime.com, **13**; © Izanoza/Dreamstime.com, **19** (left); © Macdennis/Dreamstime.
com, **21** (top); © Sharply_done/Dreamstime.com, **14**; © Ungorf/Dreamstime.com, **10**; The DW Stock Picture Library, **5** (bottom);
Erik S. Lesser/Getty Images, **5** (top); NOAA/Getty Images, **23**; Joe Polillio/Getty Images, **11**; © Jacob Carroll/iStockphoto, **18**; ©
Mike Clark/iStockphoto, **9** (bottom); © Xavier Marchant/iStockphoto, **4**; © William Stubbings/iStockphoto, **8**; © Peeter Viisimaa/
iStockphoto, **19** (right); NASA, **16** (top); Jacques Descloitres, MODIS Land Rapid Response Team, NASA/GSFC, **16** (bottom);
Jacques Descloitres, NASA/MODIS Land Rapid Response Team, Terra satellite, **29**; National Science Foundation, photo by Calee
Allen, **20**; National Science Foundation, photo by Elaine Hood, **25**; National Science Foundation, photo by Peter Rejcek, **21**
(bottom); NOAA, photo by Lt. Mike Silah, a NOAA P-3 pilot, **26**; Photolibrary © StockShot/Alamy, **9** (top); Photolibrary © www.
matthiasengelien.com/Alamy, **14**; Photolibrary/Photo Researchers, **27**; Photolibrary RF, **12**; © Mark Bond/Shutterstock, **7**; ©
George Muresan/Shutterstock, **6**; © Marek Slusarczyk/Shutterstock, **17**; © Martin Smith/Shutterstock, **15**.

While every care has been taken to trace and acknowledge copyright, the publisher tenders their apologies for any accidental
infringement where copyright has proved untraceable. Where the attempt has been unsuccessful, the publisher welcomes
nformation that would redress the situation.

1 3 5 6 4 2

Contents

Glossary Words

When a word is printed in **bold**, you can look up its meaning in the Glossary on page 31.

Weather and Climate

What is the weather like today? Is it hot, cold, wet, dry, windy, or calm? Is it icy or snowy? Is there a storm on the way? We are all interested in the weather because it makes a difference in how we feel, what we wear, and what we can do.

The weather takes place in the air, and we notice it because air is all around us.

Climate

The word *climate* describes the usual weather of a particular place. If a place usually has cold weather, then we say that place has a cold climate. If a place usually has hot weather, we say it has a hot climate.

Aircraft pilots need to know wind speed and direction, and whether it is safe to fly.

Watching Weather

People observe the weather so they can:

- make weather **forecasts**
- know what weather to expect from year to year
- warn others when there is dangerous weather on the way
- share what they have seen with others by taking photographs and making movies

Weather Measurements

One way to observe the weather is to take weather measurements. We can, for example, measure how much rain or snow has fallen.

Meteorology

The study of weather is called meteorology. Scientists who study the weather are known as meteorologists. They look at weather measurements and make weather forecasts. Meteorologists can measure the air temperature and **air pressure**. They can also measure how fast the wind is blowing, and the direction it is coming from.

Computers use weather measurements to help meteorologists track storms.

Some farmers record the highest and lowest temperatures each day.

Temperature

How hot or cold is the air? To answer this question we need to know the temperature. Temperature is measured in degrees. There are three different scales of temperature. The most common scales in use are:

- the Fahrenheit scale, which is used in the United States
- the Celsius scale, also known as the Centigrade scale, which is generally used by the rest of the world

A Comparison of Some Fahrenheit and Celsius Temperatures

Description	Celsius temperature	Fahrenheit temperature
cool day	13°	55°
warm day	25°	77°
hot day	38°	100°
freezing water	0°	32°
hot water	60°	140°
boiling water	100°	212°

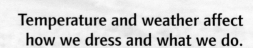

Temperature and weather affect how we dress and what we do.

6

Thermometers

Temperature is measured with a thermometer. The most common kind of thermometer is a long, thin glass tube that is closed at the top and bottom. Inside the tube is some liquid and very little air. The liquid is either mercury or colored alcohol, and most of it rests in a bulb at the bottom of the thermometer.

How Thermometers Work

When the bulb of a glass thermometer warms up, the liquid inside it expands. This makes the liquid rise up the tube. The tube has numbers marked beside it to show the temperature. When the bulb cools down, the liquid shrinks, which makes the level of the liquid in the tube go down.

Weather Report

Wind on our skin makes air seem colder than it is. The colder temperature is often called the "windchill factor."

Thermometers measure temperature. This thermometer can measure up to 122 degrees Fahrenheit (50 degrees Celsius).

Precipitation

Precipitation is the name of any water that falls from the sky. Rain, **hail**, snow, and **ice pellets** are all kinds of precipitation. We can look at weather **radar** measurements to observe precipitation. We can also use rain gauges to collect and measure all precipitation except for snow. Snow depth markers are used to show us how much snow has fallen.

Weather Radar

Weather radar is equipment that detects precipitation in the air. It also:

- works out the precipitation's speed and direction

- estimates the type of precipitation, for example, rain, hail, or snow

- forecasts the precipitation's future position and intensity

Weather radar makes maps of its observations. These maps use different colors to show the different amounts of precipitation. We can look at these maps on the Internet to see whether there is rain on the way.

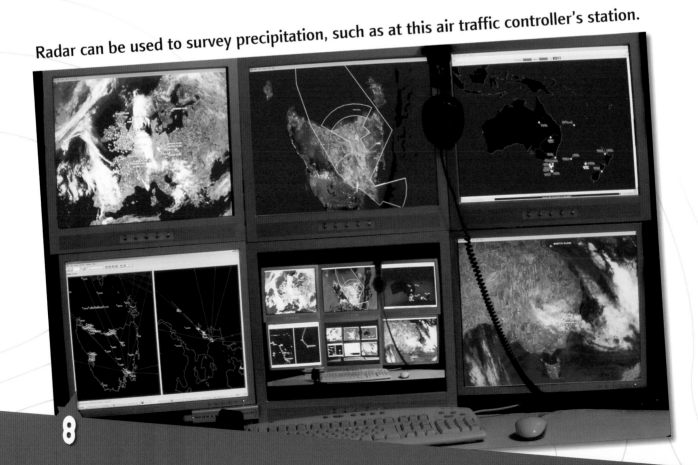

Radar can be used to survey precipitation, such as at this air traffic controller's station.

Snowfalls are measured in meters and centimeters or in feet and inches.

How Weather Radar Works

Radar equipment sends **radio waves** out into the air. These waves bounce off the water and ice in clouds. A computer works out how far away the water and ice is from the equipment by measuring how long it takes for the radio waves to bounce back to where they came from. The radar can then produce the weather maps.

Rain Gauge

A rain gauge is a container, usually a wide tube with an opening at the top so that it can collect rain or other precipitation that falls into it. It has markings down the inside that show how much water it has collected. The rainfall is measured in either millimeters or inches.

Some people have a rain gauge fixed outside their home and send their rainfall measurements to meteorologists. The meteorologists add this information to their own measurements made at **weather stations**, to get a more complete picture of the rainfall in an area.

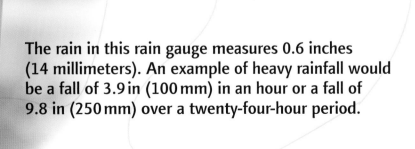

The rain in this rain gauge measures 0.6 inches (14 millimeters). An example of heavy rainfall would be a fall of 3.9 in (100 mm) in an hour or a fall of 9.8 in (250 mm) over a twenty-four-hour period.

Air Pressure

Air pressure is a measure of how much the air pushes onto the ground and on other things such as objects and people. It is measured with a barometer. We observe air pressure to forecast what the weather will be like.

A change in air pressure indicates a change in weather. If the air pressure goes down, we can expect unsettled weather in the next day or two. If the air pressure goes up, we can expect fine, calm weather.

Measuring Air Pressure

Air pressure is measured in many different units of measurement. These are:

- hectopascals
- millibars
- kilopascals
- millimeters of mercury
- inches of mercury

Aneroid Barometer

The aneroid barometer is the most common kind of barometer. Inside, it has a small metal box that contains low-pressure air. When the air pressure around the barometer rises, the walls of the box get squeezed in a little, which moves the needle attached to it. The needle points to markings that tell us the air pressure. Before we take a reading from an aneroid barometer, we need to tap it gently, so that the needle will move.

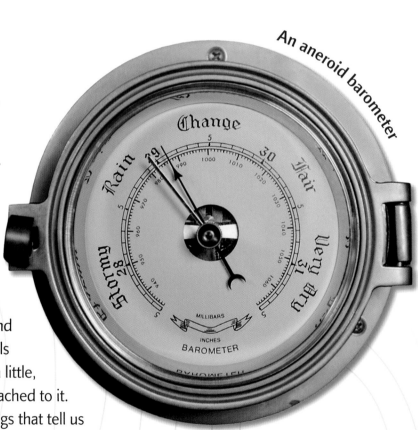

An aneroid barometer

Low-Pressure Air

Low-pressure air is thinner and has less dust in it, which makes the moon, stars, and distant objects look brighter and sharper. Low-pressure air rises, so a swamp may be smellier as gases rise. People's joints may ache more than normal as gases in their bodies expand. Sound becomes louder and clearer. The air smells fresh and clean. These things are all signs of wind, clouds, and rain.

High-Pressure Air

High-pressure air is often hazy because it has dust in it. Distant objects look a little blurred, and swamps do not smell as much as they do when the air pressure is low. When the air pressure is high, the weather is fine and sunny. Nights can be very cold because there are few clouds.

Weather Report

When air pressure goes up, more dust becomes suspended in the air. This gives us sunny, hazy skies.

Low-pressure air can make people's joints hurt, especially people who suffer from arthritis.

Humidity

Humidity is a word we use to describe how much **water vapor** is in the air.

Measuring Humidity

We measure humidity with a hygrometer. The most accurate kind of hygrometer is the wet and dry bulb thermometer. A wet and dry bulb thermometer consists of two glass thermometers. One of them has a wet cloth tied around the bulb that stays dipped in some water. The thermometer with the wet cloth on it will show a lower temperature than the dry thermometer.

The drier the air is, the more air will **evaporate** from the wet cloth, which keeps the bulb cooler. This will result in a bigger difference between the two thermometer readings. When the air is more humid, less water can evaporate from the wet cloth and the temperatures will be closer together. To figure out humidity using a wet and dry bulb thermometer, we read the two temperatures and look up the humidity on the table between the two thermometers.

The wet and dry bulb thermometer is the most accurate type of hygrometer.

Signs of Humidity

In hot weather, our skin perspires. The hot weather causes our perspiration to evaporate, which cools us down. In humid weather, our perspiration does not evaporate as easily, so we feel hotter. We also feel sticky because there is more moisture on our skin.

An increase in humidity is a sign that damp or wet weather is on the way. Some plants can give us clues about the humidity of the air. Seaweed that lies on the seashore dries out in dry air but swells and stays moist in humid air. Mature pine cones open in dry air and close in humid air. Dandelions and some other flowers open in dry air and close in humid air.

Weather Report

Singapore often has relative humidity of 100 percent. Singapore is on the equator and is surrounded by sea.

Pine cones open when the air is dry and close when it is humid.

Wind

Wind is the movement of air over Earth's surface. It is caused by differences in air pressure and the movement of Earth. Many people need to know the speed and direction of the wind.

Wind Speed

We measure wind speed with an anemometer. The simplest and most common kind of anemometer is the cup anemometer. This has three or four cups attached to a vertical pole. They spin faster as the wind blows faster.

Wind speed is often measured in kilometers or miles per hour. For boats and aircraft the wind speed is measured in **knots**. One knot is 1.15 miles per hour, or 1.85 kilometers per hour.

Wind Direction

We name the wind after the direction it comes from. For example, wind that comes from the east is called an easterly. Wind from the northwest is called a northwesterly.

Two of the most common ways to observe wind direction are with a weather vane or a wind sock.

The cup anemometer measures wind speed by measuring how fast the cups spin in the wind.

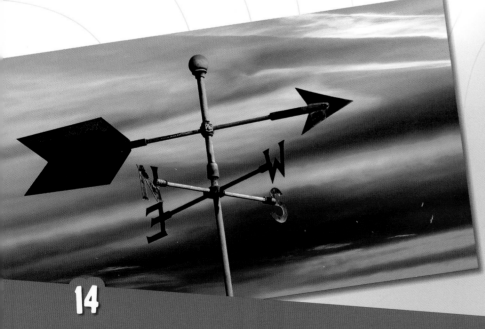

A weather vane attached to the top of a roof will show which way the wind is blowing.

Wind Strength or Force

Wind strength is a general description of the wind. A very strong wind is often called a gale, especially at sea. The Beaufort Wind Scale measures the wind speed as a force. There are twelve forces on the scale.

Watching flags blowing in the wind is an easy way to figure out wind direction.

Beaufort Wind Scale

Beaufort force	Wind speed miles (km) per hour	Wind description
0	0	calm
1	1–3 (1–6)	light air movement
2	4–7 (7–11)	slight breeze
3	8–12 (12–19)	gentle breeze
4	13–18 (20–29)	moderate breeze
5	19–25 (30–39)	fresh winds
6	26–31 (40–50)	strong winds
7	32–39 (51–62)	near gale
8	40–47 (63–75)	gale
9	48–53 (76–87)	strong gale
10	54–63 (88–102)	storm
11	64–74 (103–119)	violent storm
12	75 (120)	hurricane/cyclone

Clouds

Many people enjoy watching the clouds in the sky, and seeing what shapes they make. Clouds can often give us clues about what the weather will be like for the next few hours. Meteorologists observe clouds around the world by looking at photographs taken by weather **satellites**.

Weather Satellites

Weather satellites fly at the top of the **atmosphere**. They take photographs of clouds and beam them back to meteorologists on Earth. Meteorologists use these satellite photographs to help make weather forecasts. They also use them to track dangerous **tropical** storms.

Sunshine Recorders

A sunshine recorder is another instrument used to help measure cloud cover. The Campbell-Stokes sunshine recorder is a glass **sphere** that the Sun shines through. The Sun's rays burn a mark onto some cards below the sphere, which shows how much sunshine there has been. The more sunshine there is, the fewer the clouds.

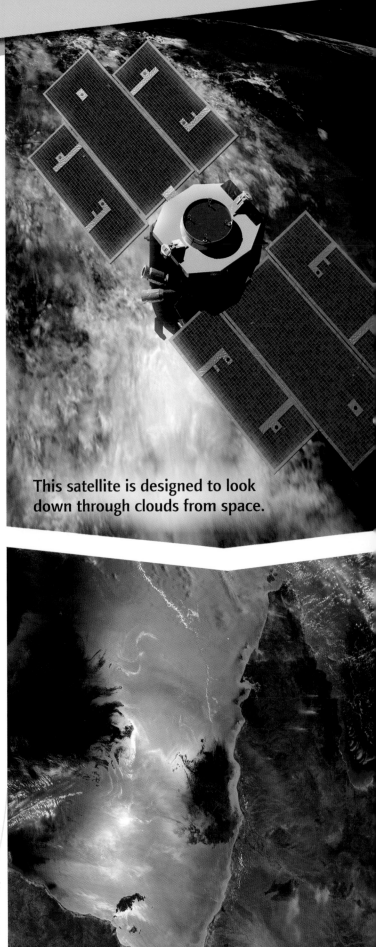

This satellite is designed to look down through clouds from space.

A satellite photo of north Queensland, Australia

Clouds Tell Us About the Weather

Different types of clouds can give us clues to the coming weather.

Cirrus Clouds

Cirrus clouds are very high in the atmosphere and are made of ice **crystals**. They often look feathery. If they are fairly thick, it may mean there is a weather front coming, bringing damp, wet, and windy weather.

Cumulonimbus Clouds

Cumulonimbus clouds are thunderclouds. They are gray at the bottom, are very tall, and have a heaped appearance. If they look close to us and we can hear thunder, it means a dangerous thunderstorm is on the way, and it is time to go indoors.

Clues that Clouds Give

These types of clouds …	come with this type of weather …
white, fluffy clouds	warm, fine weather
high ice clouds in large amounts	unsettled weather
tall, heaped clouds	possible thunderstorm with short, heavy showers
greenish thunderclouds	thunderstorm with hail
low sheet of gray cloud	damp, windy weather, probably with steady rain
no clouds, blue sky	no rain or wind, cold night ahead

Cirrus clouds are made of ice crystals and often look feathery.

Light and Colors

Lights and colors in the sky can sometimes tell us if the weather will be clear or windy, cloudy, and rainy.

Rainbows

We see rainbows when sunlight shines on raindrops in the air. In places where most weather goes from west to east, such as in most of Australia and North America, a rainbow late in the day can mean good weather is coming. This is because there are no clouds to block the Sun in the west, and the rain is passing away toward the east.

Halos and Dogs

Sometimes the Sun and Moon have thin white or colored rings around them called halos. The halos can have bright spots on them, which are called sundogs or moondogs. These are all caused by icy **cirrostratus** clouds high in the sky. They may mean damp weather is on the way.

Sun halos and sundogs are seen most commonly in areas close to Earth's **poles**, where the atmosphere is very cold.

Moon halos are caused by tiny ice crystals high in the sky.

Red Sky

The sunset or sunrise sky is redder when there is a lot of dust in the air. There is more dust when the air has high pressure. Areas with high air pressure have fine, calm weather, so dust in the air comes with good weather.

In places where weather comes from the west, a red sky in the west at sunset means good weather is on the way. A red sunrise in the east means the good weather is most likely to be passing away, and may be followed by unsettled low-pressure weather. These observations have given us sayings such as "Red sky at night, sailors delight, red sky at morning, sailors take warning."

A red Sun at sunrise or sunset is caused by dust in high-pressure air.

In places where weather comes from the west, a red sunset sky like this probably indicates dry weather is on the way.

Collecting Weather Information

Scientists use weather **instruments** to observe, record, and measure the weather. The instruments are put in:

- weather stations
- weather balloons
- weather buoys
- airplanes or satellites

The Amundsen-Scott South Pole Station, Antarctica, has collected weather information since 1956.

Weather Stations

A weather station is a place where several weather instruments are grouped together. This makes it easy for the scientists to record their measurements. Weather stations are located in cities, suburbs, and rural areas. Some people have small weather stations at their homes or at other locations, such as on boats.

Weather stations usually have instruments to measure the air temperature, air pressure, air humidity, wind speed and direction, as well as precipitation.

Weather Report

For weather observations, air temperatures are always taken in the shade, sheltered from wind.

Instruments on the Move

Scientists send instruments out to collect information about the weather. These instruments do their jobs in a number of different ways.

Weather Balloons

Weather balloons are sent into the upper atmosphere. They are fitted with an instrument called a radiosonde, which makes observations. The radiosondes record air pressure, temperature, and humidity. The balloons are tracked in order to get wind information. Weather balloons are released twice a day from eight hundred locations around the world.

Weather Buoys

Weather buoys float on the oceans. Some are tied up and others drift on ocean currents. They are linked to satellites. They record air and water temperatures, wave height, air pressure, and wind speed and direction. This information is then sent to the satellites.

Aircraft

Special aircraft send information to scientists from different levels of the atmosphere. Some planes fly right into dangerous thunderstorms—even through tropical storms.

Satellites

Satellites fly in the outer atmosphere and make observations of Earth. Some take photographs and others make **infrared** recordings, which measure heat. Satellites observe clouds, fires, sandstorms and dust storms, snow and ice cover, ocean currents, and vegetation.

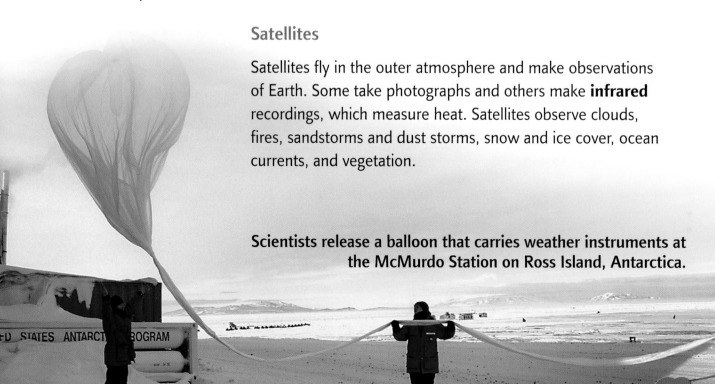

Scientists release a balloon that carries weather instruments at the McMurdo Station on Ross Island, Antarctica.

ED STATES ANTARCT ROGRAM

21

Weather Maps

People look at weather maps to see what the weather has been like over a large area, and to make weather forecasts. A weather map is a map of an area that shows weather observations for a particular period of time. Typically, a weather map will show:

- air pressure
- weather fronts
- wind
- precipitation

Air Pressure and Isobars

One of the types of information given on weather maps is air pressure. Weather maps have curved lines on them called isobars. There are small numbers written on each isobar, which give the air pressure in these places. When isobars join to make closed circles, we say there is a pressure system. A high-pressure system is marked with HIGH or H, and a low-pressure system is marked with LOW or L.

These are some of the symbols used on weather maps.

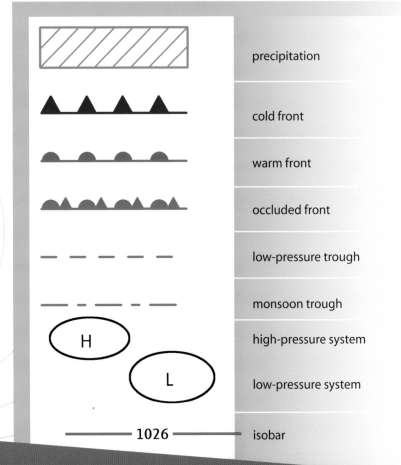

	precipitation
	cold front
	warm front
	occluded front
	low-pressure trough
	monsoon trough
H	high-pressure system
L	low-pressure system
1026	isobar

The different colors on this weather map show the amount of precipitation in different areas. The brown areas show the heaviest precipitation, and the pale gray areas show the lightest.

Weather Fronts

Large masses of air have different temperatures, humidities, and air pressures. As air masses move in the atmosphere they run into other air masses. The boundary between them is called a weather front.

Cold and Warm Fronts

A cold front is the beginning of an approaching cold air mass, and a warm front is the beginning of an approaching warm air mass. An occluded front is when a cold front overtakes a warm front and then joins with it.

Wind and Precipitation

Weather maps often show the speed of any wind and the direction it blows in. They also often show the amount of precipitation there has been over the previous few hours, or the last day. The precipitation shown is usually rain, hail, or snow.

Weather Forecasts

People can make weather forecasts to indicate what the weather will be like at some time in the future. The forecast could be for that day's weather, or for up to ten days ahead. Weather forecasts usually tell us about expected temperatures, rain or snowfalls, fog, wind, and humidity. They also warn us of storms.

Weather forecasts are made by government meteorologists, private companies, scientists, as well as everyday people. We are able to forecast the weather ourselves if we have weather maps for the last day or two.

Weather Report

Weather maps show us if a warm or cold front is on the way. This helps us know what kind of weather to expect.

Weather forecasts help people plan their day's activities

Fri	Sat	Sun	Mon	Tues	Wed	Thur
68	68	68	66	68	70	66
Shower or two. Clearing.	Showers developing. Windy.	Shower or two. Windy.	Few showers.	Mostly sunny.	Few showers.	Mostly sunny.

Weather-Map Forecasts

We can track the movement of pressure systems if we have weather maps that give information from the last day or two. These maps help us to predict where the pressure systems will probably be in the next day or so. High air pressure brings calm weather and clear skies, and low air pressure brings clouds, precipitation, and wind.

Weather maps show us the direction winds are blowing in the place we live. People usually know that wind from a certain direction will bring a certain kind of weather, so the wind direction shown on the weather map tells us what weather to expect.

Wind Direction

In the northern hemisphere, wind blows clockwise around high-pressure systems and counterclockwise around low-pressure systems. In the southern hemisphere, it is the opposite: wind blows counterclockwise around high-pressure systems and clockwise around low-pressure systems.

Computer Forecasts

Meteorologists use computers to make forecasts. They put thousands of observations from around the world into special computer programs, which then determine the forecasts.

Computers are essential in helping meteorologists prepare forecasts.

Storm Watching

Meteorologists use instruments such as weather balloons, satellites, and radar to watch out for tropical storms. There are specially built aircraft called hurricane hunters that are flown into tropical storms in order to study them. There are also people known as storm chasers who chase after thunderstorms on the ground.

Hurricane Hunters

Hurricane hunters are planes that fly right into tropical storms. They have radar on the nose and belly to measure rainfall, and radar on the tail to measure wind. The crew drop two kinds of **probes** from the plane. The probes contain instruments to measure the:

* air pressure, temperature, and humidity in the storm
* temperature of water in the ocean below

Hurricane hunters fly through a tropical storm in different directions and at different heights so all sections of the storm are observed. The crew sit at desks in the aircraft and monitor the instruments on board and the probes dropped through the storm.

These United States government aircraft are used to study tropical storms. The rear aircraft is a hurricane hunter.

Some storm chasers are trained to recognize storm clouds that may develop into tornadoes. They report these storm clouds to weather authorities, who put out a tornado warning.

Storm Chasers

People chase thunderstorms for entertainment and adventure, and because they want to share what they see by taking photographs and videos. They love to see the spectacular shapes and colors of the clouds and lightning. Storm chasing is dangerous because chasers and their cars may be struck by lightning, blown around by strong winds, and hit by large hailstones. Tornadoes can come with thunderclouds, which are very dangerous to follow because they change direction suddenly.

Weather Warnings

Many people around the world are hurt and killed by dangerous weather. Most countries have systems in place to alert people when dangerous weather is approaching.

Hurricane and Cyclone Warnings

When satellite photos show that a hurricane or cyclone has developed, meteorologists send out warnings by radio, television, newspapers, and the Internet. The meteorologists track the storm to see if it is heading for land. The warnings say what category the storm is, so that people know how severe the storm is going to be and can prepare properly.

The United States has hurricane categories for storms.

Category	Wind (miles per hour)	Surge (feet)	Effect
1	74–95	4–5	damage to some crops, trees, and mobile homes
2	96–110	6–8	damage to houses
3	111–130	9–12	houses damaged, mobile homes destroyed, flooding
4	131–155	13–18	inland flooding, houses badly damaged.
5	over 155	over 18	only large buildings remain, floods reach well inland

Australia has cyclone categories for storms.

Category	Maximum wind gust (kilometers per hour)	Effect
1	90–124	damage to some crops, trees, and mobile homes
2	125–169	minor house damage, risk of power failure
3	170–224	some building damage, power failures likely
4	225–279	buildings badly damaged, power failures
5	over 279	extremely dangerous, widespread destruction

Tornado Warnings

People are informed of tornado warnings and alerts by radio, television, and other alarm systems. Areas that experience many tornadoes usually have sirens that sound when a tornado is approaching.

Thunderstorm Warnings

All people need to be warned of approaching thunderstorms. Aircraft pilots especially need to know about them because it can be dangerous to fly in a thunderstorm.

Water Warnings

People who are out at sea in boats are given warnings if strong winds are expected. This is if strong winds—over about 26 knots—are expected. These warnings are for fishers, sailors, and anyone else out on the water.

Flood Warnings

People receive warnings when a river is going to flood, which may include how high the water will reach and when this is expected to happen. Some towns with rivers have sirens that sound when a river is rising and likely to flood.

Warnings were issued on the Gulf Coast of the United States, ahead of the arrival of Hurricane Dennis in July 2005.

Weather Wonders

The average temperature of the air at sea level is 59°F (15°C).

Cherrapunji, in India, is one of the wettest places on Earth. Its average rainfall is 450 in (11,430 mm) per year.

Some weather satellites orbit Earth at the equator, and remain above the same place on Earth's surface. Others orbit Earth over the poles.

Darwin, in northern Australia, is one of the most humid cities on Earth.

India and Thailand are two of the most humid countries on Earth.

Weather satellites are operated by the United States, Europe, India, China, Russia, and Japan.

Tropical storms are called hurricanes, cyclones, and typhoons in different countries.

Glossary

air pressure weight of the air pushing on the ground and other objects

atmosphere layer of air around Earth

buoys structures that float on water, often to mark a position

cirrostratus ice cloud that forms a flat layer

crystals pieces of pure substance

evaporate change from a liquid to a gas

forecasts predictions of something

hail falls of ice balls from thunderclouds

ice pellets ice balls formed from frozen raindrops

infrared type of energy; heat rays

instruments tools that make or take measurements

knots scale for measuring wind speed or speed of a boat; one knot is 1.15 miles per hour, or 1.85 kilometers per hour.

poles top and bottom of Earth

probes containers of instruments sent into a storm to take measurements

radar equipment that sends out signals to detect how far away something is

radio waves types of energy waves; electromagnetic energy

satellites spacecrafts that orbit Earth

sphere ball shape

tropical in the area on or near Earth's equator

water vapor water particles in the air

weather stations places with weather instruments for meteorologists to collect weather observations.

Index